This book is dedicated to the strongest woman I know my mother Sylvia S. Campbell. Because of her guidance and love throughout the years none could compare. She is truly a virtuous woman. I have learned how to live my life in a way of compassion, love and grace because I followed her as she followed our Lord & Savior Jesus Christ.

In a world where society deem people with dementia crazy or losing their minds this is not the case for one woman whose story tells things from a different point of view. Her reality is a lack of understanding why strangers are visiting her bedside, but she discovers they are not strangers. Her hallucinations will have you seeing things through the eyes of a person suffering from dementia. This book will give clarity where clarification is needed when dealing with a loved one under these circumstances.

Set your minds on things above, not on earthly things.

Colossians 3:2

CONTENTS

1. How I met the love of my life
2. The Ups and Downs of family
3. The Beginning of My Journey
4. Trying to Hold on to the Norm
5. Dressing for the Occasion
6. Strangers All Around Me
7. Trying to Remember
8. First Visitation
9. Clarification On My Condition
10. Second Visitation
11. Best Day Ever
12. Not A Good Night
13. Third And Final Visitation
14. The Day My Children Said Goodbye
15. Understanding My Point of View

Acknowledgement

In telling Sheryl's journey with dementia, it touched my heart to want an understanding of what a person with this condition must endure daily. I have often wondered what a person battling dementia see through their eyes. I thought it must be very frustrating to live in a different dimension from the actual norm. The unfortunate aspect is people with dementia are left with a different treatment from others due to lack of knowledge with others not understanding what a person endures internally. The best example is a mother who has given her whole life towards her children and then dementia happens and suddenly her whole life changes. She is constantly confused, grouchy and does not understand why her children are not around anymore. But her children are around or most of them do not know how to cope with the situation, so they stay away. But she is still there. Her mind is just confused. So, she may feel neglected and unloved because she does not understand why her children are not visiting her anymore. I want to thank God for opening my heart towards individuals who battles with dementia and to give a different perspective on how to see the world through their eyes.

One

How I Met the Love of my Life

Just in case you are wondering who I am my name is Sheryl. I am a very young attractive intelligent African American Bahamian all around woman. I never leave home without dressing up. I am a real advocate for looking your best because you never know who you may meet throughout the day. Many people leave their homes with different types of mindsets. Some people are particular about how their wardrobe match and how their hair is combed. Or others may leave home in their bedroom wardrobe without a care of others judging their looks. I was the one who carefully overlooked my whole appearance before anybody saw these hips. I mean, if you got it why not show it! You know what I mean?! Well anyways, my house had no more food, so I decided to go grocery shopping. As I walked down the aisles, I notice a handsome gentleman smiling my way. So, I decided to smile back because he was so cute. He had a body built to last like a FORD. I mean this guy could probably get any woman he wants. His skin was golden brown like honey, and he had a look of certainty within himself. "You know it is very disrespectful to stare at someone without speaking," I said while approaching him. "Oh really?" He responded while smiling. "Yes really!" I responded while doing my flirtatious smile. He said, "Well, I am imagining my future life with the beautiful lady in my view." I said, "Which beautiful lady?" Of course, I knew he was talking about this sexy young lady right here. Well, hello beautiful, my name is Calvin Remington. And what is your name? (While extending his hand towards my hand.) My name is Sheryl. Nice to meet you, Sheryl. How would you like to become Mrs. Sheryl Remington? I felt like I was being swept off my feet. I had to clutch my pearls. How could I say no to such a handsome gentleman. Usually, the gentleman would have to ask your father for permission to have your hand in marriage, but unfortunately, my father died when I was 12 years old. He left one morning to go to work and died while working on the job. My mother said she heard footsteps in the house later that evening and thought it was my dad returning home. She realized it was nobody, but then she received a phone call about my father's death. I remember crying so much because I really loved my father. He was a cool dad. He showed me everything I needed to learn, and he always treated me like a young lady. Even though I was only 12 years old when my father died, he showed me how I should be treated by a boy. I replied, "I Do not know you at all Mr. Calvin Remington, but I would love to learn more about the person you are." He said, "And I would love to learn more about the person you are too!" (With a silly sly grin on his face.) We exchanged phone numbers, and the rest is history. On my wedding day I wore a beautiful white gown made from the most beautiful material you could ever imagine. Calvin had on a handsome tuxedo. As the minister officiates our wedding the camera is on Calvin as he smiles and say his vows while placing the wedding ring on my finger. I felt like a queen. I was told by the minister to say my vows to Calvin. So, I basically told him what I expected him to do for me for the rest of our lives. And he laughed but agreed to what I was offering. I placed the wedding ring on his finger. The minister holds up his arms and said, "I now pronounce you husband and wife. You may now kiss your bride." We both embraced each other with a kiss. As my family cheers for us we ran to our vehicle which was decorated with wedding bells hanging from the bumper and a sign in the back window saying, "Just Married." As we drove away, I could hear people screaming and cheering us on our journey. It did not take long before I was pregnant with my first child. She was a beautiful baby girl, and I named her Lora. As Calvin stood by my bedside in the hospital delivery room, I felt like everything was going to be ok. As I proceeded to go into labor, Calvin is by my side encouraging me to breathe. The nurses were monitoring my contractions as the doctor proceeds into delivery position in front of my legs. I was in so much pain but eventually, I was able to push out my baby girl. A year later I was pregnant again. Calvin is smiling with excitement but looks nervous about baby number two. Eventually, I went into labor and a baby boy was born and we named him Calvin Jr. He was a handsome little fellow. We had a family of four and I thought we were finish. Well, a year later I was pregnant again. Calvin was looking for a chair to rest in because he was overwhelmed. He could not believe what the doctor informed him about me being pregnant again. Eventually, I gave birth to another little girl, and we named her Stephanie. She was another beautiful baby girl. Eventually, I became pregnant again with baby number four. When I was going through this pregnancy, I started bleeding badly and by the look on Calvin's face I knew he felt sorry for me. As the doctor approaches, Calvin begins to comfort me and guides me into a room. Moments later I am in labor, but my baby was still born. Unfortunately, this will be one of four different pregnancies of still born or miscarriages. I was pregnant ten more times. The children names are David, Peter, Seth, Greyson, Steven, Marc and a set of twins named Tina and Stina. When the twins were born Calvin shouts out a dramatic scream with excitement. (While breathing hard.) I was very weak but overjoyed with the two for one special. Two babies during one pregnancy were incredible. Three years later I am pregnant again with a baby boy. We decided to name him Jerome. Calvin swings his arms signaling no more children. I am the one doing all the work during these pregnancies and deliveries, and he is swinging his arms as if his body was traumatized, not mines. Another three years later I am pregnant again. This time it's a baby girl and we named her Lyla. As Calvin held her in his arms he smiled. By the look on his face, you could see how much he adored his precious little bundle of joy. He bends over and kiss my cheek as he cuddled our newborn baby girl. Can you imagine having a house full of kids?! Oh my gosh, we had our own little league. Calvin and I are tries to maintain our thirteen children from changing diapers to taking them baths in addition to feeding them and putting them to bed. Then you must make sure they all are dressed and ready for school. There was never a dull moment in the Remington's home.

Two
The Ups and Downs of Family

As time passed our oldest daughter Lora begins dating and eventually gets engaged. All my sons were in her wedding, so they all needed tuxedos. As they traveled to the tuxedo store the weather was very rainy and the roadways were slippery with a lot of construction. Calvin Jr. was 23 years old at the time and he was driving. David was 16 years old, and Peter was 15 years old. They were both in the back seat. Suddenly Calvin Jr. loses control of the vehicle and their car flips over the roadway. David and Peter were both rushed to the hospital. My heart skipped a beat when an officer came knocking at our front door informing us of the accident. We rushed to the hospital as quickly as possible. It was one of the longest rides I have ever endured. The doctor enters the room where my two boys are laying in their hospital beds, and he begins to speak with us concerning their inability to walk again. We are informed they are both paralyzed from the waist down. As Calvin and I gather around their hospital beds we are feeling hurt and pain. I mean who wants to hear of their children not being able to walk again. We have always been Christians, and we believed God for healing, but we are grateful for our sons not losing their lives. It still made us cry for hours. I hugged my two boys and comforted them the best I could.

As I aged my life became full of motherhood with no room for friendships and due to the children & the number of responsibilities I started having seizures. Eventually I was diagnosed with epilepsy as the doctor showed an x-ray of a tumor on my brain. I can see Calvin is overwhelmed but continues to do the best he can as a husband and as a father. He is such an awesome man. My mother tries to fulfill her role as a grandmother the best she can.

She has always been a loving and caring mother. One day my mother came over and she was assisting me due to my health challenges. As we were talking, she suddenly lost use of her legs and collapse by my bed side. She died leaving me and my sister Ruth behind. A couple of years later my son David was trying to remove him-self from his wheelchair and fell on the hard floor. After a couple of weeks his face started to swell, and it begin to look bad. We took him to the doctor's office. The doctor placed an order for an x-ray of the jaw. Once the results came in the doctor showed us a tumor growing in his jawbone. The doctor informed us David has jawbone cancer and it had metastasized. Words cannot explain what I was feeling in that moment. It seemed like there was one thing after another. It was very frustrating because I did not understand why all of this was happening to our family, but my trust in God never wavered. As the weeks and months past David started looking small and weak. There was an over-sized knot on the right side of his face, and it caused a skin infection. David died five months after his diagnoses. My baby boy was gone and there was nothing I could do about it. My heart sunk in my chest. The Remington's family circle was now broken.

A couple of years later my husband starts feeling sick as he bends over while cutting the grass. I thought maybe he was having bad gas or a common stomachache. The pain was constant and was not improving with over-the-counter medication. I told him he needs to see a doctor. He agreed and we made an appointment. As we visited the doctor, he wanted to examine Calvin's stomach. He ordered a CT scan (a medical imaging technique that uses X-rays and a computer to create detailed pictures of the inside of the body) and a Pet-scan (a nuclear imaging test that uses a radioactive tracer to show how well the body's organs and tissues are working). The doctor told us to wait in his office as he collected the results. The doctor returns with a look of disappointment and I knew the news would be bad. Calvin was diagnosed with stage four liver cancer (the most advanced stage of liver cancer, when the cancer has spread from the liver to other parts of the body).

I watched my husband change from a strong well independent man to this skinny health challenged individual who could not stand on his own two feet. I felt so hopeless, and I did not know what the future hold for me and my children. My husband died six months after he was diagnosed with liver cancer. When he died a part of me died and I was a little lost with anger. I mean how dare he leaves me here by myself with all these children! I was angry, I was hurt and, I was confused as to why God allowed this to happen to me. My sister Ruth came to live with me so she can assist with overseeing the children.

Ruth and I are close. We did everything together. Although she and I had many fights over who was the prettiest. Yes, of course, I was but she figured my beauty came from her since she was the oldest. We would run around the beautiful fields of our home because we grew up on a beautiful island. It was surrounded by blue ocean water and some of the best views of nature. One day Ruth was in the room playing with my youngest daughter Lyla and suddenly she had a heart attack falling over to her death. Once again, I was faced with a harsh reality of losing someone close to my heart. After all these unfortunate encounters my life begin to involve just me and my children.

Three
The Beginning of My Journey

In the rest of my years of living as a single mother I have learned to enjoy life with my remaining twelve children. They have grown into the greatness of what Calvin, and I have taught them over the years. I miss Calvin every day. At first it was a challenge not seeing him around or not being able to have his assistance in my everyday life, but he has taught our children well enough to manage our bills and finances. My youngest daughter Lyla was blessed with a house of her own. She built it in Georgia which is about eleven hours from where I live. Every summer we would take a road trip to visit her house which is currently a vacation home since my baby girl still lives close to her mother. I have already packed all my clothes because Lyla told me she was on her way. I still cannot believe how much she has grown into this independent woman. It appears she notices how lonely I have become since all my children have grown into their careers. Sometimes the house is so quiet until I hear voices whispering but of course this is impossible because I am the only one home. Tina and Marc still live here but they are always at work or out running errands. As I waited for her to pick me up, I was reminiscing of the time she was just a baby in my arms. She was so chubby and vibrant. Calvin took her everywhere he went. She was like his little road buddy and never left his side; However, whenever I was cooking, she never left my side either. She would just stand there waiting for breakfast, lunch, or dinner to be served. Most kids would have to be called, but not Lyla. She was waiting for the food to be ready. That was my baby girl. Now she is all grown up and driving me to her new vacation home. On the other hand, Tina one of my twin daughters became my right-hand help. She went away to college and after she graduated, she came back home. I am so happy she decided to stay with me because I noticed a change with my thinking pattern. Nothing drastic, but the chores in my everyday life became a little difficult to maintain. I did not want to alarm anyone because it was a little embarrassing. I was always independent, and I considered myself the "biotic woman!" Yes, that very sexy independent lady who had the tv show called, "Wonder Woman." I mean there was nothing she could not do! This woman was machine, and no one could ever beat her at fighting. She would spin around in a circle and suddenly, a magic rope would appear around her waist, and she also changed into a sexy custom. If you ever made her mad, you better run if you see her starting to spin in a circle. Yep, that was me the "biotic woman." But this day I did not feel assured of myself. Tina would often assist with packing my luggage for my road trips and she would always make sure I use the restroom before hitting the road. Once Lyla arrived to pick me up, I was ready to ride on the road. I loved the sight-seeing on our journeys because it reminded me of the beautiful nature God had created. I love the Lord because He kept me through all my life, and He made sure I had enough children with Calvin so they would be around to take care of me after Calvin was gone. The Lord knew He would take Calvin home with Him and I would need some assistance. One of my other sons Marc was also home to assist Tina with my everyday care. Between the two of them I was always looked after while relaxing at home. Before Lyla and I left for our road trip, Tina wanted to join hands and pray for safe travels. I smiled inside because Calvin and I always taught our children to pray. It did my heart good to see my children understanding the importance of prayer. As Tina led us out in prayer, we all joined hands in agreement. Once we were done praying it was time for Lyla and me to start our road trip. One of my favorite parts of road trips are the different eating spots we traveled through like "Steak n Shake." My favorite sandwich is the Frisco burger. Yummy to my tummy. I have never tasted any other burger like it. We finally arrived at Lyla's house, and I remember sitting on her couch. As I was sitting there, I remember thinking how beautiful her house was, but I was feeling tired and exhausted. I blanked out and when I woke up, I was in a hospital. I thought, "What is going on?!" I was confused and disoriented. I remembered traveling with Lyla to Georgia and arriving at her house. But what was I doing in a hospital? I felt a little tired and weak. At first, I was still confused and wondered who the four young men were standing next to my hospital bed. Apparently, Lyla called her four brothers who previously relocated to Georgia. All my sons look like their handsome father. Each one of them shared a special characteristic of Calvin. Peter had Calvin's stern personality and the fact that he was in the wheelchair did not hinder this strong personality. If you did not want to hear the painful truth, do not ask him because he would tell you the truth even if it hurts. Then there is Seth who had his father's confidence. No matter what the situation was Seth was never wrong about anything. He was right even when he wasn't. I chuckled inside whenever he would have arguments with his brothers. Steven was more of an athlete and would often join any type of physical sports. He also loved music and is musically talented. Calvin Jr was more laid back and mature than the others. He had to help his father with finances throughout the years so his younger siblings would have the necessities of life. He had his father's wisdom to work and save his money. He also managed to purchase many properties just like his father taught him. Apparently, I had two seizures back-to-back once arriving to Georgia. He stated the long road trip may have caused the shock to my body but said everything else looked normal. He did not notice any signs of a stroke or a tumor. A nice nurse came in to check on me and she looked like a candidate for one of my sons. Peter to be exact because Seth is already spoken for with his wife of many years with four beautiful children. The nurse looked like she was flirting with Peter because he had the biggest smile upon his face. It was obvious she wanted to make sure my sons knew she had my health as her best interest at heart. She made sure all my vitals were in good standings and my ability to understand who she was and why she was checking on me. I was feeling hungry and wanted to drink some hot tea along with a sandwich. She gladly agreed and asked Peter if he wanted or needed anything as well. I guess she could care less about my other three sons in the room. Of course, there was some smiling going on but maybe it was just my imagination because I was still feeling weird inside my body & mind. Eventually, I felt my body falling asleep. As we prepared to return home to Florida, I felt fine and comfortable. Lyla decided to travel at night so the traffic will be without many cars. I thought it was a great idea. I was sitting in the passenger seat and suddenly, I was in church telling other church members how good God has been to me. It felt so good being in church again. The excitement of praising God is so powerful. As I thought about the many surgeries and injuries, I had to endure it's hard not to get excited about how God kept me through all of it. It is like the most powerful feeling. I mean when I think about the many times I could have died, it made me cry. I am still alive and able to walk on my own two feet. My daughter kept asking me if I was ok. I did not know why she kept bothering me. I thought to myself, why is Lyla asking me if I'm okay. Of course, I am okay. I am celebrating with other believers about how good God has been to me. My daughter kept looking at me like she was confused about something. I don't know what her issue was but if I am being honest, it was very ignoring. After a while, I noticed we were still on the road, but there were strangers riding in the back seat of the car. These strangers looked creepy. They had faces that looked like creatures. Their eyes were big and red. Their mouths were huge with large teeth. They were forming at the mouth and their hands looked like claws. They were trying to grab me out of the front seat. I just needed to get out of the car and as far away as possible. My daughter was trying to pull me back from opening the car door. I thought to myself, "Why is she trying to keep me back from escaping these crazy/scary looking creatures?" The next thing I knew the car finally stopped. Once I got out of the car my baby inside of my womb was putting pressure on my bladder. It felt like I was going to give birth at any given moment. I kept trying to tell my daughter we needed to hurry because the baby is coming. As I started rushing towards the restroom at the truck stop, she started pulling me back towards the car. Eventually, I saw the nurse standing and waiting for me to come towards her direction. But as I approached her, she looked suspicious. Her eyes were small and sharp. She had an evil look on her face like she wanted to harm my baby. I felt like she wanted to steal my baby away from me. I tried to tell my daughter, but she kept looking at me like I was speaking another language. Then I noticed a police officer walking over towards the nurse. They were both pointing at me as if I had done something wrong. My daughter insisted that everything was okay, and she will make sure me and my baby were safe enough to enter the building for the restroom and delivery. What was interesting was how confused my daughter was during my plea for help. And it was very frustrating because all I wanted was to feel safe. Everything seemed confusing and scary all in one.

Four
Trying To Hold on To the Norm

My husband Calvin built a beautiful big house with plenty of stairs. Our master bedroom is located on the 3rd floor. As time passed, it became difficult to climb the stairs. I did not want Tina or Marc to worry about me so I kept a blanket and pillow on the couch downstairs so I can have a comfortable spot to sleep at night. My daughter Lyla would come by some evenings and one evening she decided to sit with me until I was ready to go to bed. I kept telling her it was okay for her to go home. I insisted I will be ok, but I guess she noticed I was falling asleep while sitting on the couch. After her persistence I had no choice but to inform her of my difficulties with transitioning up and down the stairs. I mean, after all I am supposed to be the "biotic woman." I have always been independent and never needed anyone's help or assistance. Regardless of how much pain I was feeling my response to anyone asking how I am doing; it would always be I am doing fine but deep down inside I was not doing fine. One of my ways of escaping my true feelings was through gardening. Whenever I was outside in my garden, that was my time to reflect and talk to God. It was very refreshing because out there was fresh air and beautiful plants, flowers, and trees. Nothing frustrating will ever enter that atmosphere. I am remembering one time when my son Greyson decided to pay me a visit. He was so handsome like his father. Everything about him reminded me of the younger version of Calvin. Greyson always felt like he was supposed to take care of me after his father died. Any and everything I needed came through him. He was the appointed caretaker of Calvin's properties and financial occurrences. He and his wife had three handsome sons. There would be moments, I had to refer to their nicknames due to each of their personalities. I loved my grandchildren to the moon and back, but let's just say their nicknames are Hurricane, Tornado and Thunderstorm. Okay! Now you can imagine or figure out the rest. I loved my talks with Greyson and would often ask him about my daughter-in-law. He would joke and say, "She is at home, and I better get there before she thinks I am out cheating on her." We both laughed because we knew how she would jokingly accuse him of coming home late due to extramarital affairs. She was a beautiful young lady with a heart of gold. She loved my son with all her heart. The special bond within their marriage was so evident. I loved her as if she was one of my daughters and I believe she loved me as a mother.

Five
Dressing for the Occasion

Once again, I am trying to complete a task, but it seems harder to do. I was simply trying to get dress for church, but I kept having a hard time. One minute I knew what I was going to wear and how I wanted to fix my hair. But then as I am preparing to dress up, my mind would go blank, and I would be trying to figure out what it was I was trying to do and what task I was trying to complete. One of my twin daughters Stina was always good at coordinating the perfect outfits for any occasion. She also knew how to fix hair in a special way. Every time she assists me with dressing up for church, everyone would compliment my outfits and hairstyles. My daughter knew her stuff and I would just smile at the many compliments. Inside I thought, boy if y'all only knew it was not my doing, but my mini-me. Listen, whenever I entered the sanctuary, heads turned and notice my nice apparel. The girl has style, and her mama taught her well. Eventually it was Christmas time and on Christmas we always celebrated Calvin's birthday. Even after his death we continued the celebration. During this time, I would also dress up in my beautiful evening gown because beautiful is what I represent (if you have not figured it out.) I mean I was dressed down to the core. The house was decorated in beautiful white Christmas lights and decorations. Our house was the brightest one in the neighborhood. Many people would drive by just to see the lights. There were people everywhere. The music was playing, and people were dancing. The grandkids said their speeches, some danced and some sang their songs. It made me smile so much until my face started to pain from the cold weather. The tears rolling down did not help with the uncomfortable feeling.

Anytime we had our Christmas celebrations, I always felt a need to thank God for long life. One of my favorite scriptures in the bible is Psalm 118:17 "For I shall not die, but live, and declare the works of the Lord!" I also wanted to thank everyone for coming out and celebrating Christmas Eve with the Remington's family. My husband and I loved celebrating Christmas with our thirteen beautiful children! My baby boy Jerome wrote a song called, "Sunday Morning!" The words to the song tells the story of how we conducted ourselves here at the Remington's home. In my heart I have always wanted to warn people of my Lord and Savior Jesus Christ soon to return for the ones who are saved. My favorite saying is "Hell is still smoking, and God is not joking!" My guests would laugh, but I was serious about what I was saying. As time passed, I started forgetting things easily. Eventually it was hard for me to take my own baths and my ability to walk became more difficult to achieve. Eventually, I could not stand on my own two feet. It felt very depressing because it affected my independence. I mean, not only did it take away my ability to walk around my home, but it also affected my ability to drive. My life changed drastically as this disease called, "Dementia" begins to deteriorate my mind, body and soul. It appears nothing will ever be the same. I felt like a different person no matter how hard I tried to stop my body from changing. I remembered when I took care of myself, my husband and my thirteen children while cooking and cleaning. Things were a lot easier when I was younger, but my body started changing. I could feel pain in every joint, muscle and anything within my body. Mentally, I felt a shift and there was nothing I could do to stop it. My mind started playing tricks on me. One day I tried to explain to my son Marc that I was not feeling well, and he asked me was my stomach hurting, I said no. He asked me was my head hurting and I said no. It was weird because I did not have any symptoms of sickness, I just did not feel like myself. I mean a little arthritis, but that was it. I felt a shift within my mind. An unexplainable shift of confusion, uncertainty, and uncontrollable doubt. As I tried to explain my feelings to my son Marc, it became evident he did not fully understand what was causing my sickness. Eventually weird people started visiting me and this was not the way I thought my life to turn out.

Six
Strangers All Around Me

As time passed some strange lady started coming in my room telling me things she was going to do for me. I mean the nerve of some people coming in your personal space. Every time I looked up, she was smiling in my face like we are buddies. I don't know who this lady is and why she is in my bedroom. Somebody has got some serious explaining to do. If it was not the strange lady, it was some girl coming inside my room calling me mama. I am looking at her like she is not my daughter. Or could she be pretending to be my daughter. I did not know how to feel about all these changes. I wanted things to go back to normal, but every day it got worse. I did not know how to express my feelings so I would just scream and shout. They would look at me as if I was crazy or something. And I was looking at them the same exact way because I knew who I was, but I did not know who they were. Then this grown man walks in my room without even opening his mouth to say good morning. I am looking at him and he is looking at me. I asked him if he did not know how to open his mouth and say good morning! His response to me was good morning mama. Here we go again with somebody calling me their mama. I looked at him and my response was uh huh. I mean what else does he expect from me. Well, whoever they were it helped that I was carried to the toilet because I could not walk. I appreciated the help. I only wish I knew who they were. They also gave me a bath and made sure I was all cleaned up before placing me back into my bed. The bed I was laying in was not like a normal bed. It would raise my back or my legs into a comfortable position. Then there was this feeling of some type of balloon like mattress underneath my body. They would turn my body sideways and lay this long pillow along my backside. It felt good whenever they changed my body position because laying in one position caused my body to become stiff. After a while this strange lady was trying to feed me some food, but I do not trust strange people feeding me. She may try to poison me with something bad causing me to become sick. I just knocked that spoon out of her hand because I don't know her like that. I mean, she looked okay, but bad people look okay too. And then they do the unthinkable and then you are dead. I just trust the people I am familiar with. But this lady was very persistent. She kept trying to feed me something from a bowl and I kept knocking the spoon out of her hand. I told her no! I did not want whatever she was trying to feed me. As I held my head down, I was very frustrated and mad. I felt like I was a stranger in a strange land. All these strangers kept coming in and out of my room. But when I lift up my head, my sister Ruth was standing beside my bed! I was so happy and glad to see someone familiar. I begin to cry because I haven't seen my sister in a long time. She was smiling and she looked very young and pretty. I missed her so much. Everything I was feeling or thinking she understood and would give me the best solution for solving any situation. She asked me were that strange lady bothering me. I told her I guess not, but the fact that she is a stranger bothers me. I mean why is a stranger trying to take care of me? I would rather see her, or mommy or daddy take care of me. And every time I wake up, I am in the same room laying in the same bed. I never get to go outside to my garden, and it is driving me crazy! My sister understood exactly how I was feeling and offered to feed me some of my breakfast. I was so glad she offered because I was hungry, but I did not trust that strange lady feeding me. Once she fed me breakfast, I started to feel sleepy. Next thing I knew I was in la-la land dreaming away. I found myself in a beautiful field of green grass everywhere. The flowers were big and colorful. There was hills and hills of fresh flowers everywhere. Whenever I moved it was like I was running fast. I felt the breeze hitting my face and it was cool. As I approached the top of the hill, I heard a whistling sound. It got louder and louder the closer I got to the top. Once I reached the top of the hill there was a deep blue ocean. The water was so blue it looked like it was fake. As far as the ocean ran there was pink sand all around it. There were not any trash or people on this beautiful beach. There were not any trees hiding the view. The birds were flying high above the sky, and I felt so calm. I never wanted to leave. The place was heaven to me, and I enjoyed my time. I thought it would be great if I could stay there forever. It was better than laying in a hospital bed all day while different strangers ask if everything was alright. Every time they asked that dumb question, I wanted to scream because it should be obvious how things were for me. I mean, I was bedridden, and my own children were not around me all the time. Again, I kept seeing different strangers walk in and out of my personal space. I wish I had rocks so I can pop them upside the head so they would leave me alone. I am not a mean person. I just want things to return to normal. Apparently, I am in a different world. Nothing seems the same and everyone keeps looking at me like I am crazy or something. My days are long and boring because no one familiar ever stops by. It is always these strangers asking me am I ok. I am thinking maybe I have been abducted by aliens. They took me to another planet where everything looks similar, but it is not my home. I have people calling me mom and they look at me with signs of worrying. Maybe I can just sleep forever and never wake up. At least I will not have to worry about living in a strange land. I can sleep forever and enjoy my rest. That will be heaven for me. I wish I can walk again and work in my garden. Those days were therapy to my soul. I even started walking for cardio and stress relaxation. One of these days I will be in heaven, and I will run wherever I wanted to go. Yes, that will be a joyous day!

Seven
Trying to Remember

Another day of laying in my bed and in walks a young lady. She is very beautiful, but I do not recognize her face. I had to ask her who she was because again all these strange people keep entering my room. She told me she was my daughter named Lora. Well, my daughter Lora use to be a small little girl with ponytails. This strange lady was telling me she came by to check on me. I figured since she is telling me that she is my daughter, I wanted to share with her about my sister Ruth coming by to visit. Although, while I was talking, she had a confused look on her face. I was telling her how we spoke for a long time and how she fed me breakfast. But she said my sister died many years ago. That really made me upset because if Ruth was dead, I would not have seen her the other day. I know who I saw, and she was smiling at me, and we talked for a long time. I told her how much I missed her and everything. Why is this lady saying my sister died years ago?! That really upset me because I saw Ruth with my own two eyes. I told her nobody died! I wanted her to get that through her thick skull! I mean, how dare she says something as mean as that?! Something so hurtful and disrespectful?! Then in walks this other lady giving me a kiss on my forehead talking about, "Hey mama!" Talking about she just wanted to show me some love. Then she asked that dumb question everyone keeps asking, "How are you feeling?" I just looked at her. Then I figured since she is calling me mama, she must have known my sister Ruth. I told her how I saw my sister the other day and she responded with the same thing the other lady was saying. She said my sister died years ago. Listen, if I was not so weak, I would have stood up and smacked her straight in her mouth for saying that about my sister! I told her she was standing right by my bedside. I figured she did not hear me, so I repeated my words with a louder voice. I guess she heard me the second time because she said "okay" and she believed what I was saying, and she was glad Ruth came to see me. I told her I was glad too because I miss her so much. She barely visits me anymore. It was like she suddenly stops coming to my house. I am thinking maybe I made her mad or something, but the last time I saw her she seemed happy and smiling. I do not know what is keeping her away from me. We used to be very close and now she is never around. Maybe it was something I did. Sometimes, I do things out of order, and it is not intentional. I mean, I was always known for my slick feisty attitude and no matter what the situation was, I was never wrong. Everyone else was wrong and I was always right. At least in my eyes, I was always correct. Everyone else just needed to get with the program. I mean, I knew who I was and whatever I say goes. No matter the situation, I am always right. After all I was the "biotic woman", and she is never wrong!

Eight
First Visitation

After a long day of laying in my bed doing nothing all day it started getting dark outside and I felt my body falling asleep. When I opened my eyes there was a male figure standing at the foot of my bed. I said hello and he said hi. I could barely see his face, but his voice sounded familiar. I asked him what he is doing in my bedroom, and he said he was checking on me. I told him I was doing ok, but I did not like the fact of not being able to walk around anymore. I also told him how I miss walking in the park and doing gardening. He begins telling me a story about when I was a little girl how I loved playing outside. He said I was always doing something to help my mother since I was the baby in the family. He said my older sister was always doing other things, but I was always next to my mother watching and helping her complete her tasks. After rubbing my eyes and listening to his voice I realized it was my father. I hadn't seen my papa since I was twelve years old. I could not believe it was my papa. I missed him so much. As he smiled at me, he confirmed that he was my father. Once he came closer, I saw his face a lot clearer. He looked very young and handsome. I begin to tell him how I missed him so much and how things changed in my life. I told him how mom was sad all the time. He told me how sorry he was for leaving us the way he did. He said he never planned to leave that way, but he guesses God had another plan. I started crying and begging him not to ever leave me again. I told him I wanted to go with him because I was not happy with my life. He told me in time I will be able to come with him, but for now he must go. He told me he will always be watching over me. He said I had grown into a beautiful woman. He looked like he was tearing up and was so proud of me. I started crying more and I had to accept him leaving me once again. Then he disappeared from my bedroom. I know he said I could not go with him, but I figured if I screamed and cried loud maybe he would change his mind, but it did not work. My son came inside my room asking me if I was ok. I figured he was my son because he called me mama. He looked worried and confused as if he did not understand why I was screaming and crying. I was trying to tell him I wanted my daddy, but he kept looking at me like I was crazy, and he kept telling me his grandfather died a long time ago when I was a little girl. I told him my father was standing by my bed a few minutes before he came in my room. I was so hysterical from crying and screaming till I felt my body shaking from screaming so much. He is telling me no one is standing by my bedside. I am thinking to myself, "Duh, he is not standing there now, but he was standing there before you came in my room!" I screamed to the top of my voice telling him yes, he was standing right over there! My father was standing over there talking to me!" Apparently, he finally believed me and begin to tell me everything was going to be alright. I never thought anything would be wrong! I just knew I missed my father, and I wanted to go with him wherever he was going, but once again he left me behind. It hurt badly and I could not stop crying. I must have cried myself to sleep.

Nine
Clarification On My Condition

Apparently, I had to go see some man about how I was feeling because he kept asking me all kinds of personal health questions. There were some other people with me that looked like my children. These people would often call me mama and seem to care for me a lot. I felt fine that day. For some reason my body was not aching, and my spirits were positive. I mean, I was still unable to walk around and do whatever I wanted to do, but I guess the fact of getting out of my bed to go somewhere made me feel better. Once we got to some place we had to wait outside with other people. Eventually, some lady dressed in all white called my name and someone pushed me in my wheelchair to another area. She took me to an area where another man was, and he was wearing all white as well. He was checking all my body parts and asking me all kinds of dumb questions. Sometimes, I stared at him with aggravation because I got tired of people asking me the same stupid questions. He is asking me things like do I know my name and do I know where I am. I mean, honestly, I did not know the answers, but the questions were still dumb to me. I wanted to be left alone and not asked so many questions all the time. Next thing I knew they were all sitting in one area talking. Eventually, one of them said, Ma, are you ready to go?" I am assuming it was my daughter because she called me ma. I am thinking what she thinks?! Does she think I love sitting in a wheelchair over in a corner while they all talked about me? I heard some of what the man in all white was telling the other people. He said something about me having a condition called "Dementia." Apparently, it causes me to act mean sometimes and nice at other times. They were all complaining to the man in white about how I was being mean to them all the time. He explained to them that this thing called Dementia makes me act that way sometimes. I also heard him say that I may see things that's not present. Then one of them asked me if I was ready to go home. I said, (with a blank stare) "What you think?!" And they all started laughing at me like I was some kind of comedian. I was looking at them like is there a clown in the room or something? I do not know what to think of everything. I just knew I was ready to leave because it was cold and unfamiliar.

Ten
Second Visitation

There I was minding my own business laying in my bed. I can tell it was bedtime because it was dark outside. Those people who are always calling me mama came in to tell me goodnight and I could not really sleep. Whenever I cannot fall asleep, I just stare into my bedroom. As I was laying in my bed, I heard a baby crying. A beautiful lady all dressed in white approached my bedside, but she does not say a word. At first it scared me because she was holding something in her arms. As she got closer, I noticed a small baby in her arms. The baby was dressed in a little white gown, and it kept crying. I asked her why is the baby crying? The lady stared at me without saying a word. I asked her if she wanted me to hold the baby so I can try to stop her from crying. The lady just stood there. I heard someone come in my room and it must have been my daughter because she called me ma. She asked me what I was doing, and I told her I was trying to help the lady stop the baby from crying. My daughter asked me if I needed any help, and I told her I did not think so. And then I proceeded trying to quiet the baby and calm it down. I said, "Its ok little baby, mommy and I are right here. I told the lady how beautiful she was and how beautiful her baby is too. She gave the baby to me so I could hold her. When she gave me the baby, the baby stopped crying. When I looked down into the baby's face it started smiling at me. It was a beautiful baby girl. I asked the lady what her baby's name was, and she smiled and said, "This is not my baby girl." I was so confused because if the baby was not hers, then whose baby, was it? And why did this lady have someone else baby in her arms? I was thinking maybe that is why the baby was crying because she took it from somebody else. So, I asked her what she meant by the baby not being hers. I said, "You brought me this crying baby!" She replied (While smiling), "Yes, I did, but this is not my baby. It's your baby girl you loss during one of your many pregnancies. As I heard the words that was coming from her mouth, my mind begins to remember for just a moment. I remembered being pregnant, but the baby was still born. As I recalled this horrific event, tears begin to fall down my face. I looked at the beautiful baby girl once more and begin to accept the fact that she was my little girl. That was one of the most painful experiences in my life. I never thought I would be able to get through those painful memories. As I looked up at the beautiful lady and asked, (for confirmation of what I just heard) "You mean this is my little Casey?" The lady replied, "Yes, it is." I said, "Wow, she is so beautiful. I was wondering how I was able to stop her from crying." The beautiful lady replied, "Yep! Moms always know what's best for their babies." She had a smile on her face, and she said, "I wanted her to see her mom for a little while." I told her thank you and that she can leave her with me. She said, "I wish I could, but she must go back with me. You will see her again soon." I started crying and rocking my baby slowly in my arms. The lady proceeded to take the baby away from my arms. I figured, if I screamed loud, she would let the baby go and leave her in my arms. So, I shouted to the top of my lungs and screamed, "No! Don't take my baby away from me! Stop it! What are you doing?!" Somehow, she was able to pry the baby out of my arms and slowly walked away. I just continued screaming hysterically and this other lady is calling me mama and telling me everything is going to be okay. I thought I was going to lose my mind. This lady (whose apparently my daughter because she called me mama) is telling me everything is going to be okay while I am trying to get my baby back from this other lady. I screamed and screamed until I could not scream anymore. It was like I lost my baby all over again and I had to re-live the pain I felt when she was still born. I thought to myself, "Whoever that lady was dressed in all white, the next time I see her she will get a good beat down "biotic woman" style. I thought to myself, "she just doesn't know who she is messing with by taking my baby away from me! I mean the nerve of some people!" I felt strong and weak at the same time. I felt strong enough to whoop her behind, but weak enough to cry like a defeated woman.

Eleven
Best Day Ever

The sun was shining brightly this day. I knew this because this was the day I spent outside. The girl that keeps calling me mama (in which I am guessing she is my daughter) decided to take me outside for a scroll. I felt good and I was in great spirits. I did not have an episode in weeks and slept well most nights. My daughter made a comment about how beautiful the day was, and I agreed. Again, the sun was shining bright, and the birds were singing their songs. I loved it out there and the garden was so pretty. I had some flashbacks of working in it. It seemed so peaceful and graceful being around the flowers and plants. Someone else joined in on our conversation and she also called me mama. She was telling me how she was just finishing work and decided to stop by so she can check on me. She gave me a hug and it was like I knew she was my twin baby girl, and the other girl was her twin. Sometimes, I have moments when I know who my children are and can feel their presence all around me. But other times they are strangers to me. I do not know how to communicate with them on how I am feeling. Sometimes I feel like they don't love me anymore and sometimes I feel like who are they and why should they care so much for me? Things are very confusing at times. But I am loving the way it smells outside. Nothing like fresh air to do a body some good. Staying in a bed cooped up in a room all day is no fun. I mean, I know being outside in the sun too long may harm my body, but I miss it so much. I told my daughter I do not want to ever go back inside. She said I cannot stay out there forever in the hot sun because I can become dehydrated from all the heat. She said we can stay for one more hour and then we had to return inside unless I wanted to return right now. I looked at her so hard as if to say you know I am not ready to go back inside. And then I said, "You better not take me inside!" I do not know why they are always laughing at me as if I'm some kind of comedian or something. I am a serious woman and when I say something, I mean what I say, and I say what I mean! But they just keep laughing at me. Then she said the doctor said I cannot be outside too long. I replied, "I guess so, if we have to return inside that is fine." After all I was in a good mood so any type of hanging outside was great in my book. We laughed and talked about many things. I really enjoyed the time I spent with these two girls. As the evening draw near, one of them said she had to leave and the one who usually checks on me all the time said it was time for us to return inside. Even though I was sad about going back inside, I cherish the time we spent together because it was the best day ever!

Twelve
Not a Good Night

I was laying in my bed, and I felt something wet. I did not feel any pain or anything, but it was kind of uncomfortable laying a wet bed. This lady who is always calling me mama walked in and was acting frantic because I guess she did not like what she saw in my bed. I heard her on the phone with 911 emergency and she was telling them how there was a brown liquid in my bed, and it looked bad. Next thing I knew there was some guys dressed in a uniform asking me all kinds of dumb questions and telling me they were going to take me to the hospital. Again, I felt fine. I mean, I was fatigued, but no nausea or anything like that. As we arrived at this place that looks like a hospital someone came and placed me in a bed (apparently with wheels because they proceeded to push me into another room). Next thing I know I fell asleep. When I woke up, I felt a sharp pain in my stomach. It was very uncomfortable. I heard my daughter's voice, and she told me she was just checking my stomach. Then I heard a man call me mama and it sounded like my son Greyson. I am glad I am recognizing my children voices. Then I heard another different woman voice who sounded like my daughter Lora. She told me all my children were there and all of them was not allowed to come inside my room. I was too weak to respond, but I wanted them to know I was happy to hear that they were all there so I smiled the best I could. Later I heard someone (a stranger voice) telling me I just had an operation, and a feeding tube was placed into my stomach. I was listening but wondering what they meant by a feeding tube. They continued telling me everything will be fine, and I can still eat through my mouth (if I desired), but the feeding tube will be accessible as well. I was thinking these people have lost their minds.

Why would I need a feeding tube if I can still eat through my mouth?! Just a bunch of dummies aggravating my soul. Just that quick, I wanted to smack each one of them looking in my face! I am guessing a couple of days later; I was transported back home to my own bedroom. It seemed like all these different people kept visiting my bedroom calling me mama and asking me if I was ok. After a while, I got use to talking to all of them. I guess it was kind of cool seeing all these different people call me mom. They must really care for this beautiful lady. I mean why would they wonder if I was doing ok? I mean, after all I am the "biotic woman", and nothing can keep me down. I have been through a lot of things, but I am still here, although many people do not understand how to communicate with me. Or maybe I do not know how to communicate with them. I know when I scream or bald up my fist they move faster. That is the best communicating from me to them. I promise, I never did it to be mean, it was just frustrating and aggravating. I would try to tell them what I needed or wanted, and they would be looking at me as if they couldn't understand why I was making the sounds I was making. And then whenever I would try to tell them about my sister visiting, or my father visiting or when the pretty lady brought my baby girl for a visit and took her back; they would look at me as if I was going crazy or something. I did not like being looked upon that way. It made me feel quite uncomfortable and almost defeated. I mean, if the people who called me mom could not believe what I was telling them, then why would a stranger believe me. I felt so stupid at times. Sometimes, I would not speak for days because I felt like what's the use. They will just look at me and respond with some dumb questions. I don't know. Maybe it's best for me to just give up and sleep forever.

Thirteen
Third And Final Visitation

I was asleep in my room when suddenly I was awakened by a male figure standing on the side of my bed. As I rubbed my eyes, I realized it was Calvin. My handsome husband all dressed in white. He had the most attractive clothing on. He looked so peaceful, and he had a smile on his face. He said, "Hey beautiful." I asked him was it really him. And he said, "Yes" (as he smiled.) He asked me how I was feeling, and I felt fine, so I told him I was feeling fine. And then I asked him how he was feeling, and he said he was feeling happy. And I asked him why he is so happy? And he said, "Because." I said, "Because what?" Because I was confused on what he meant by because. He said, "Because I finally get to spend the rest of my life with you." I said, "Really?!" I mean, I was so confused because somehow, I remembered he died years ago. But he smiled and said, "Yep!" As I sat up from laying in my bed, I took his hand. I asked him how I was able to sit up without assistance. He said, "Because you are with me now." As he smiled, he said come and walk with me, because he wanted to show me something. He led me out of my bedroom and into a beautiful house. The house looked almost the same as my original house, but it had a much bigger view. I said, "This is a beautiful home. Whose house are we in?" He asked me if I liked it. I said, "I love it!" Suddenly, I heard a voice calling out from one of the rooms. It sounded like a familiar voice. When I looked up it was my son David. Somehow, I remembered he had died from "jawbone cancer" years ago. I did not understand how he was right there in front of me, and he was not in a wheelchair. He came and gave me a big hug. I said, "David is that you?!" He replied, "Yes ma'am." (With the biggest smile on his face.) I was thinking how this is even possible. I felt confused, but happy. David's face looked fine. Calvin told me to come with him because there was more to see. David said he will see me when I comeback with his father. I'm like, "Uh ok!" As Calvin led me further into this beautiful house, I heard another familiar voice. It sounded like my dad. He always called me "baby girl." I yelled, "Daddy! Is it really you?!" He said, "Yes, it's me! I ran and gave him the biggest hug. Then I heard a woman's voice from behind me and when I turned around it was my mother. I yelled, "Hi mom!" I felt like a little girl all over again. I was crying tears of joy. Calvin said, "Come on beautiful, I have one more room to show you." As we approached the room, I could hear young children voices. As we entered the room, there were four young children playing. I asked Calvin who these kids are in the room. Calvin said, "Remember our four little ones we loss during pregnancies, well these are them." Suddenly, my knees felt weak as I fell to the ground weeping with tears of joy. It was all so overwhelming. As I begin to wipe the tears from my eyes, I asked Calvin what is this place? He said, "This beautiful place is our eternal home." As I turned and looked around, I notice a huge glass window with a view of the backyard. There was a woman standing with her back turned towards me, so it was hard to see her face. I asked Calvin who was that lady standing in the backyard. Of course, with his slick mouth he says, "Why don't you go outside and see for yourself?!" I wanted to pop him upside the head, but I knew he was being Calvin. I mean, this is why I loved him so much. Although, he can be so playful at times. As I approached the woman, I notice a familiar shape. Once I arrived closer to the woman the lady turned around and it was my sister Ruth! I screamed so loudly that whatever birds were around flew off so fast. I must have scared all of God's creation. I jumped, hugged, and squeezed my sister's neck so tight until she could hardly breathe. She said, "Hey baby sis! I see you finally made it! (With the biggest smile on her face.) I told her how much I missed her, and Calvin came out to join us. We all smiled at each other and as I turned my attention towards the direction Ruth was looking there was miles and miles of a clear blue ocean with pink sand on the beach. The ocean reminded me of the island I grew up on as a little girl running and collecting shells. At last, my whole world felt complete, and I was finally back to the norm. No longer was I living a nightmare of strangers flooding my personal space. I was finally home with a family I knew so well, and boy was I happy!

Fourteen
The Day My Children Said Goodbye

As I watched my children gather around the old me, they all looked so beautifully dressed. All my sons were dressed in black suits and ties. All my daughters were wearing black dresses. The music was playing as each one of them laid a white rose upon my casket. Eventually, it was my youngest baby girl Lyla turns to place her rose on top of my casket, but she broke down in tears looking up at me in the sky. My daughters, Lora, Stephanie, Tina and Stina, and my sons, Greyson, Calvin Jr., Peter (who rolls his wheelchair up), Seth, Steven, Marc, and Jerome all hug in one big circle as my baby girl Lyla finally releases her rose. When I saw them down there, I wanted to tell them not to worry about me. I wanted to tell them I am fine and am with their father and their brother and their grandparents and aunt. I wanted to tell them about the beautiful huge house that we are living in and about their other brothers and sisters and about the beautiful ocean view in the backyard. I wanted to tell them I am so happy now that I am back to normal. I wanted to tell them how sorry I was for not being able to communicate my feelings. I wanted to tell them that I love them and how one day we will all be together again. You see no one would ever understand what I was feeling inside. The best way I can describe it is my life situation was simply "My Story to Tell."

Fifteen
Understanding My Point of View

If your family member or anyone you know is suffering

from dementia remember they are still inside there.

Please try to treat them the same way you would want to

be treated because in their eyes you are still expected to

be there for them as if nothing has ever changed. ~

Sincerely,

Mrs. Sheryl Remington

Made in the USA
Middletown, DE
14 January 2025

69144508R00047